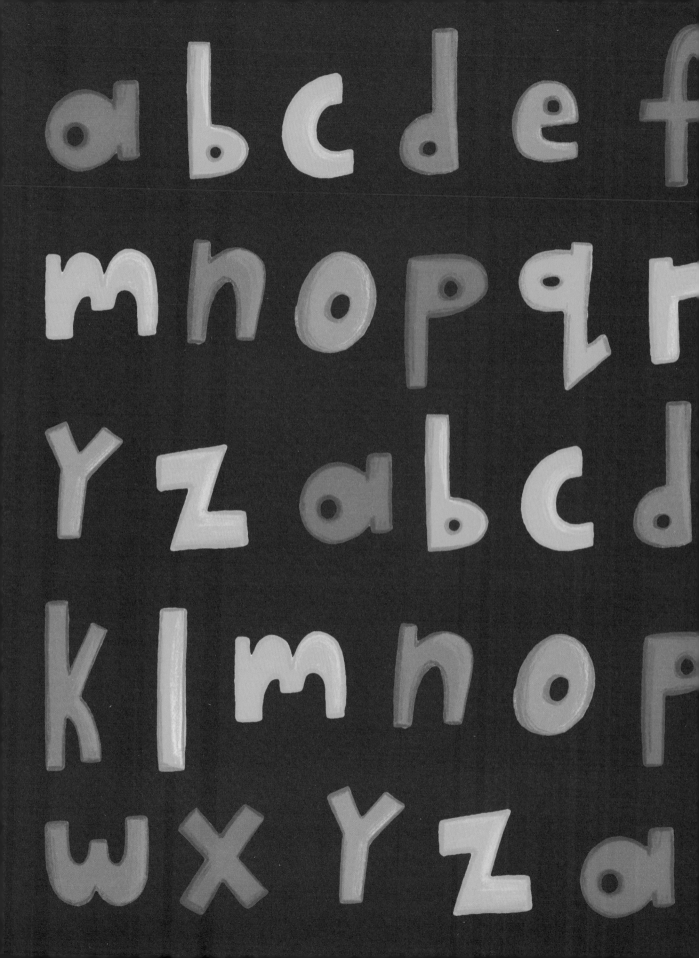

The LITTLE i WHO LOST His DoT

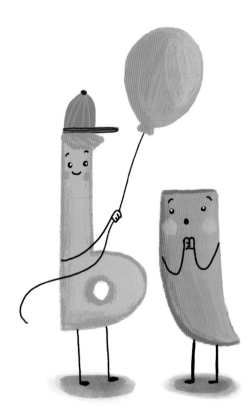

To My Children and
Children Everywhere.
—K. G.

To Mom and Dad.
—S. S.

Published by Familius LLC, www.familius.com

Familius books are available at special discounts for bulk purchases, whether for sales promotions or for family or corporate use. For more information, contact Familius Sales at 559-876-2170 or email orders@familius.com.

Library of Congress Cataloging-in-Publication Data
2018937135   pISBN 9781641700160   eISBN 9781641700634

10 9 8 7 6 5 4 3 2 1

First Edition

Printed in China

The LITTLE i WHO LOST His DOT

KIMBERLEE GARD

illustrations by

SANDIE SONKE

FAMILIUS

A... B... C... D... E... F ... G... The alarm clock rang to the alphabet song.

Little i sat up, stretched, and rubbed his eyes. "Last day of Alphabet School!"

He saw his letter friends on the playground and hurried to join them. Little g gasped, Little p pointed, and Little s stared. "Little i," they said, "where is your dot?"

Little i looked up.

He looked to the left.

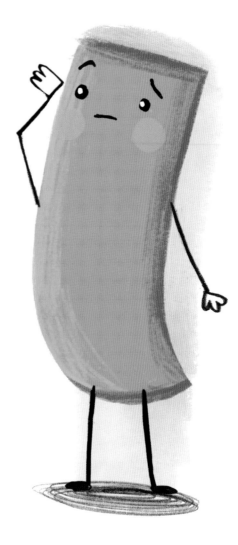

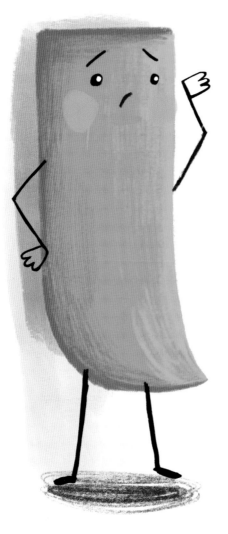

He looked to the right. But his dot was gone.

"What will you do
without your dot?"
Little a asked.

Little w
whimpered.
Little h handed
her a hankie.

All of the letters crowded around Little i.
"Don't worry," they said. "We'll help you find
a new dot."

The school bell rang. It was time to make words. All the little letters scrambled into school, but Little i's friends didn't forget their plan. When they got to the classroom, the letters looked around.

Little a asked, "How about this acorn?"

Little b burst forward
with a balloon.

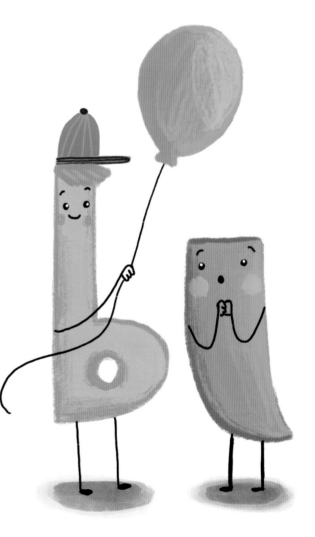

Little c cried,
"Try on this clock."

Little d dashed over
with a donut.

Little e exclaimed, "An egg is exactly what you need!"
Little f followed with a flower.

Little g giggled when
he found a gumball.

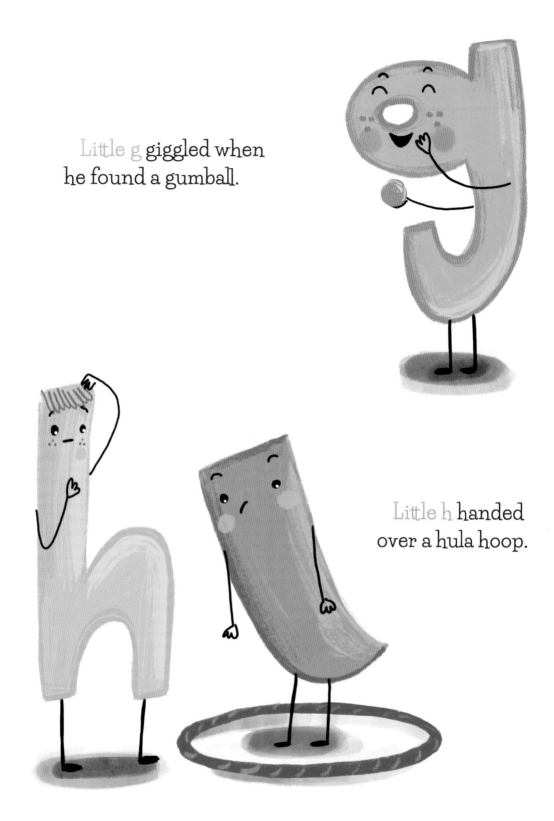

Little h handed
over a hula hoop.

Little j joked, "How about a jumping bean?"

Little k knew the answer: "A kiwi."

Little l lit the line with a light bulb.
Little m made her way over with a marble.

Little n
nodded to a
music note.

Little o opted
for an oyster
shell.

Little p presented a pretzel.
Little q questioned, "How about this quarter?"

Little r raced over with a ring.

Little s scared him with a spider.

Little t thought a
thumbtack would do.

Little u urged him to carry an umbrella.

Little v ventured forward with a valentine.

Little w walked over with a wheel.

Little x's eXtra
special idea was a
xylophone mallet.

Little y yelled,
"Wear this yo-yo!"

Little z, always last, zoomed over with a zero.

Little i tried them all on, but nothing felt right.

When school
ended, all the little
letters went out to
where their parents
were gathered.

Little i saw his father and sniffed back tears. "I lost my dot."

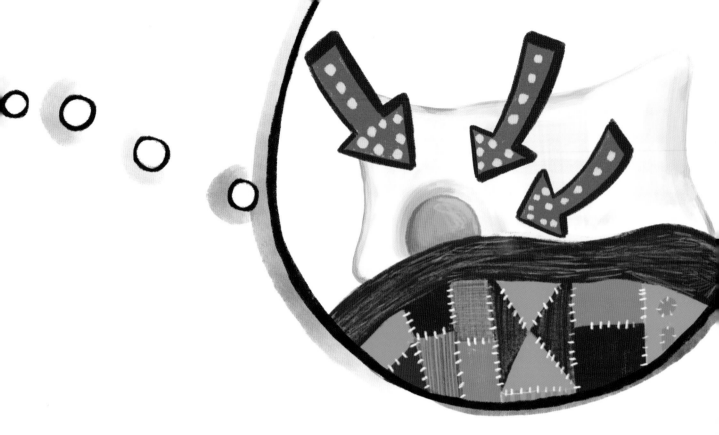

Capital I smiled. "No, Little i, you didn't lose your dot. You left it on your pillow this morning. I brought it along, but since today is the last day of school and you've grown up, I'm not sure you need it anymore. What do you think?"

"Do you really think I'm ready to be a big I?"

Capital I nodded. "Stretch out your arms and point out your feet."

Little i did, and when he saw his shadow on the ground, he smiled. "Dad, I look just like you! I can start a sentence now!"

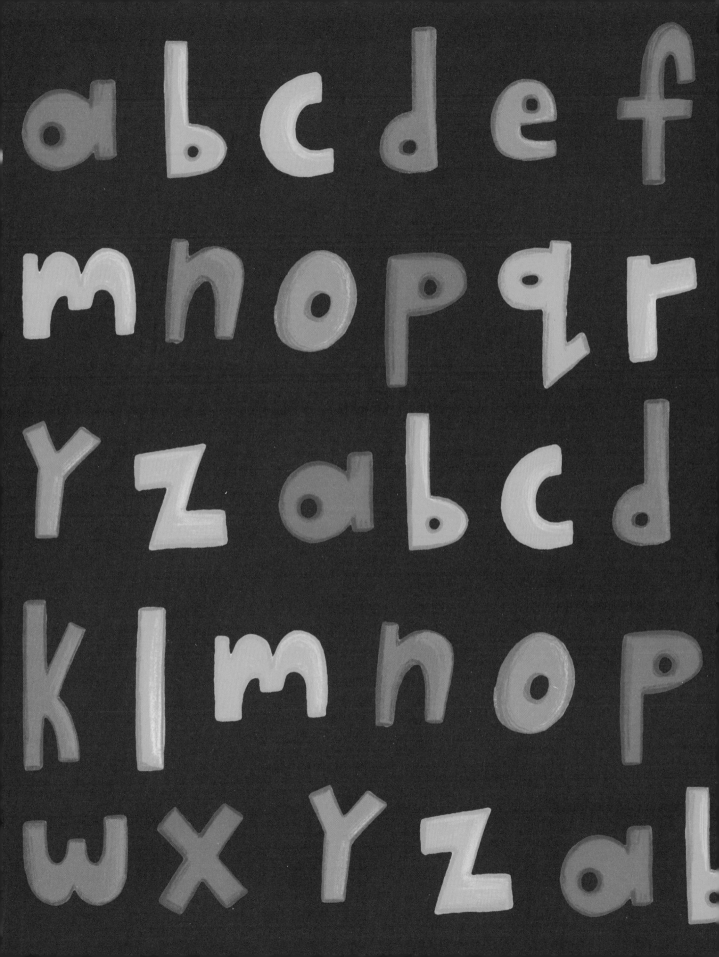

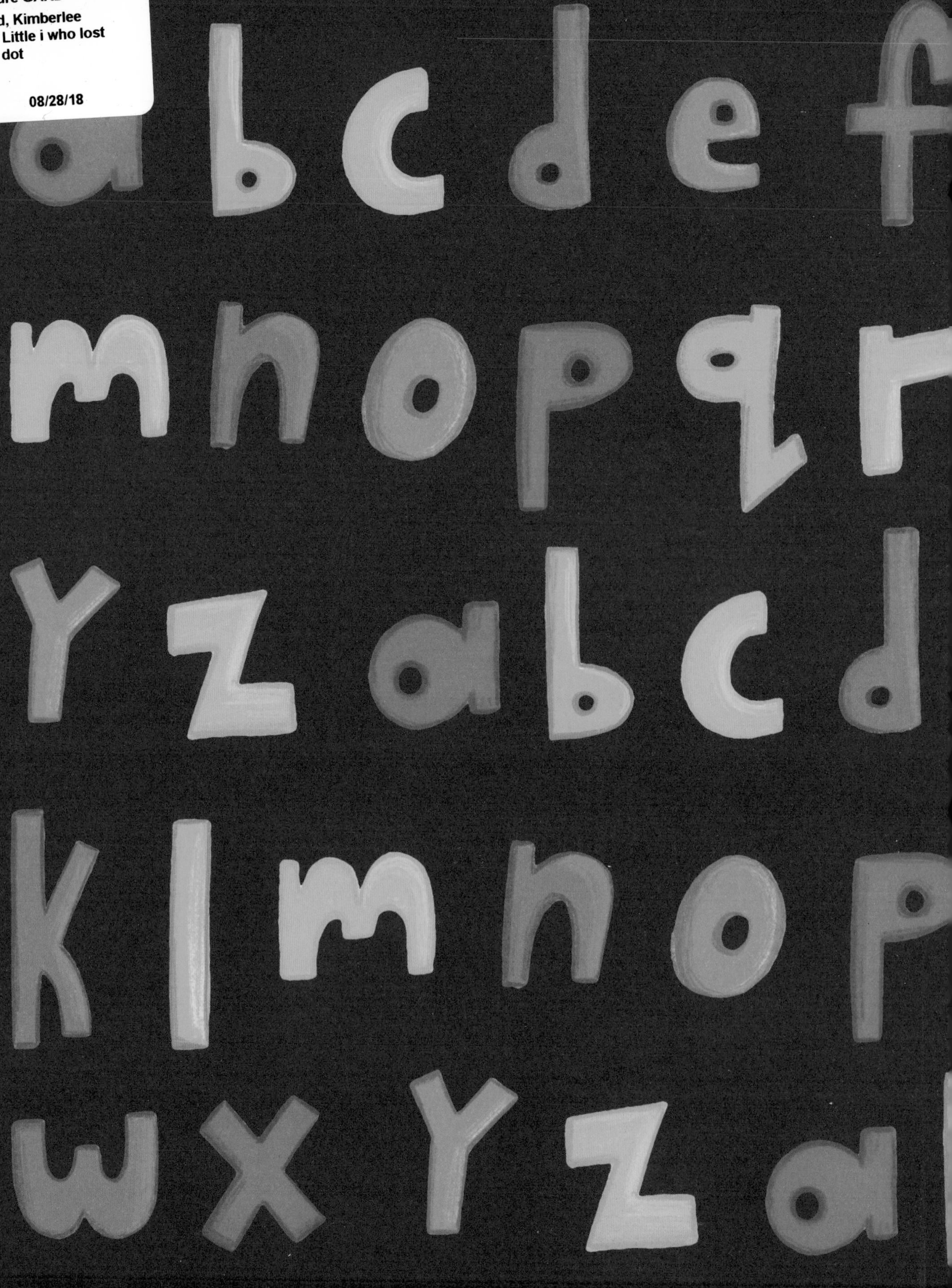